The Adventures of

SUPERMANNY

"Through My Eyes"

Written By: Holly Bueno

Illustrated by Tiffany Tutti

First published by Dog Ear Publishing
4011 Vincennes Rd
Indianapolis, IN 46268
www.dogearpublishing.net

ISBN: 978-1-4575-4304-3

This book is printed on acid-free paper.

This book is a work of fiction. Places, events, and situations in this book are purely fictional and any resemblance to actual persons, living or dead, is coincidental.

Printed in the United States of America

For my littlest super heroes: Skyler, Ariana, and Supermanny.
You can do anything you put your mind to.

And, for my husband, Manny, because I promised

you one day you would see our son walk.

Thank you for always encouraging me to make

my own dreams a reality. You truly are **MY HERO.***

WOOSH!

The world is seen through our minds, not only our eyes. So, the world as I see it, is very different from the way you see it.

And that is MY super power.

When I feel Mommy dress me in the morning,

I know she is gently sliding the clothes onto

my body *for* me.

But, the way I see it, I can do it all

by myself. I feel myself pulling my shirt over

my head, and I smile at my messy hair in the

mirror. I feel my fingers button my cape

around my neck on the first try.

When I see Daddy starting up my feeding

machine, my mind sees that I am sitting

at the table, stronger than ever. I can cut

pancakes into tiny shapes with my fork.

I feel the syrup ooze out of the bottle.

And I giggle while I lick the sticky sweet goo

off my fingers.

When the bus driver rolls me onto the bus ramp before school, I see myself climbing the 3 stair steps all by myself. My backpack is slung over my shoulder and I turn around just in time to wave and yell back, "Bye, Mommy!"

When I look out the bus window from my wheelchair, I prefer to think I am sharing a seat with my best friend, and we talk about our favorite superheroes the whole time.

When I get to school, I work really hard. I have all kinds of therapists and nurses. Every single one of them reminds me I am the coolest hero of them all.

I wish I could hug them and remind them that they work just as hard as I do. And I cannot thank them enough. So, I smile, and somehow they hear me loud and clear, because they smile right back.

After school, I may be rolled up a ramp into my house, but I see myself bursting through the doors on two strong legs, eager to tell Mommy and Daddy all about my day at preschool:

That I watched my friends climb trees, and I saw myself up there on the highest

branch!

That they talked to me, and I heard my

strong voice answering with my own words.

And that my friends asked me if I wanted to

play, and I saw myself jumping off my

seat and racing the kids to the baseball field.

When I get home, my sisters build with blocks next to me on the floor. I imagine I am adding the final piece, completing the tower. Then, they cheer, because I helped!

They push me around and spin me in my chair. I imagine I am twirling on my own with my cape flying so awesomely behind me.

When I look at my action figures lined up on my dresser, I imagine bringing them to life with my own two hands. I watch them soar through the room, crashing and swooping with my very own sound effects.

When I look at my side-kick (my puppy) who

loyally stays by my side, I know that one

day I will learn to whistle and throw a ball

for him. I will laugh as I watch him run it

back to me over and over again.

One day I will walk.

One day I will high-five my dad.

One day I will tell my sisters how much I

love it when they talk to me.

One day I will fly.

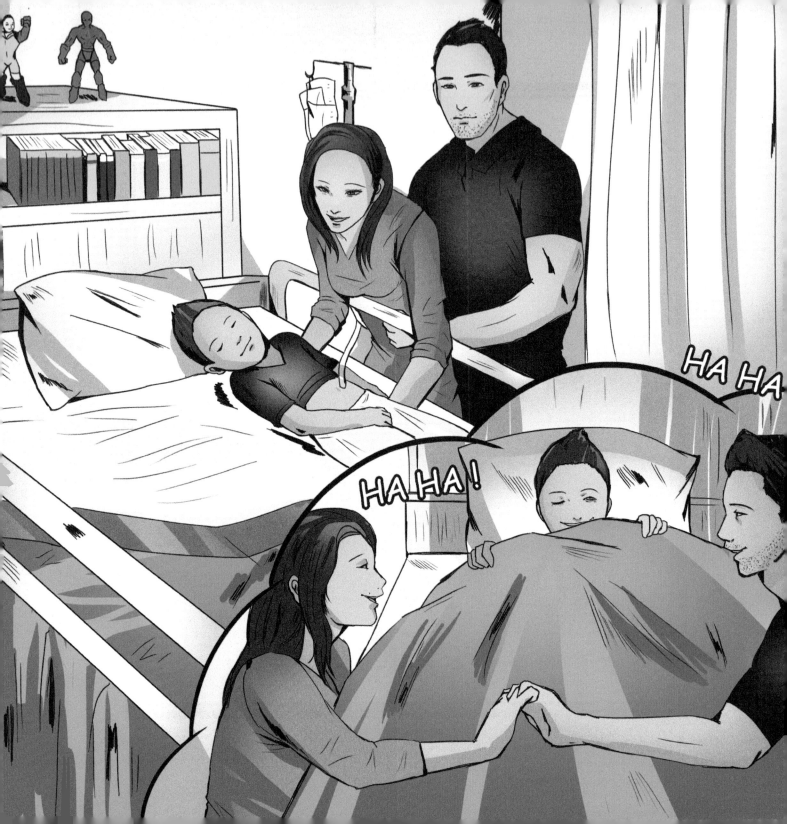

When I go to bed at night, I feel Mommy and

Daddy lay my tired body down and tuck me in.

But, in my mind, I am jumping into bed,

rolling the covers over my head, and playing

peek-a-boo with them as they laugh and kiss

me goodnight.

Mommy and Daddy always say,

"I love you,
my little super hero."

And, even though I know I may never get a

chance to say it out loud, I always hear

myself whisper back,

"I love you, too."

Our greatness is not limited by our disability;

it is measured by our ABILITY.

The world is ours to be seen through our

minds, our hearts, and our greatest desires.

And *that* is the

greatest super power

of them all.

How to utilize this book:

Supermanny may have Cerebral Palsy, but Cerebral Palsy does not have him.
Here are some ways to create positive discussions with your child and loved ones:

M When reading this story to your loved one, encourage them to describe how they can relate to Supermanny.

- How do you envision doing daily activities in your mind?

- In what ways do you dream of making tasks easier or more fun?

- How does Supermanny's day compare to yours?

M Encourage siblings to see what an impact their interactions make on children who cannot express their thoughts the way they do.

M Remind family that Cerebral Palsy comes in all levels of impairment and to *never* underestimate their disability OR their ABILITY.

M Smiles, interactions, inclusion, and conversations go a long way. Remember that the inability to speak and move is *not* the same as an inability to think and feel.

Remind loved ones that asking questions to better understand the child's disability is encouraged and respected. Make every moment a teachable one.

 No two children have the same journey with Cerebral Palsy. It should never be viewed as a negative experience. Encourage your children to see the beauty in differences and find ways to celebrate those differences as a team.

 Living with a child with a physical impairment can be difficult. Remember that siblings are constantly watching the way you, the caretaker (aka Superhero), handle stressful situations. They will learn how to handle difficult circumstances by watching your actions and reactions. Show them how to help. And, more importantly, never be afraid or ashamed to ask for help. Even superheroes need a break from time to time.

What is Cerebral Palsy (CP)?

According to the Cerebral Palsy Foundation, CEREBRAL refers to the brain. PALSY refers to the loss or impairment of motor function. There are many forms of CP: Spastic, Dyskinetic, Ataxic, and mixed. The most common form of CP is Spastic. This is where muscles are tighter and movement is affected. That can happen to different parts of the body. Some experience spasticity on one side of their body (left or right) as well as upper or lower extremities. The type of Cerebral Palsy Supermanny has been diagnosed with, for example, is Quadriplegic Spastic. This means muscles from all four limbs (legs and arms) are affected.

The Cerebral Palsy Foundation maintains that most people with CP will walk. 60% will walk without the use of an aid, 10% will walk with an aid, and 30% will use a wheelchair. Furthermore, 1 in 5 people with CP will have communication difficulties. If you are like Supermanny, then you will require a wheelchair, and you communicate through your eyes and your smile. That is pretty special!

Resources:

To learn more about Supermanny's real life journey and to see pictures of Supermanny and his family and friends, or to learn how to help, please visit www.healingsupermanny.com or

follow us on Facebook at www.facebook.com/healingsupermanny or

on Instagram at www.instagram.com/healing_supermanny

Supermanny is a hero to other children with special needs! In 2016, Supermanny will begin helping ATI Foundation raise money to help other kids just like him through the Supermanny Mission 5k (Formerly known as the Supermanny Shuffle)! To find out more about ATI Foundation, the 5k, and to see if you can be a candidate for assistance, visit www.atipt.com

Hyperbaric Oxygen therapy has been one of the most influential ways Supermanny has found healing with his traumatic brain injury. To learn more about this type of therapy, visit www.midwesthbot.com

Other great resources for information and services can be found at www.yourcpf.org or www.easterseals.com

CPSIA information can be obtained
at www.ICGtesting.com
Printed in the USA
LVOW05s2248090116

469891LV00005B/7/P